FARMING

In the world today there are many different kinds of farms. Some farms only grow crops like oats, wheat and barley. These are called arable farms. Other farms just keep animals like cows, pigs, sheep and chickens. Some farms keep crops and animals, and these are called mixed farms. But wherever the farm and whatever it grows or raises, you can be sure that the farmer works hard all the year round, so that most of us have enough to eat and drink. Find out about these different farms, what the farmer does in spring, summer, autumn and winter, and why the government gets involved in making farming laws. You can also learn about different farm animals – how they live and how they have their young. There's also a farming argument for you to think about in this Young Puffin Fact Book which brings farming to your front door!

Libby Purves has written and edited several books, but this is her first one for Puffin. She presents Radio 4's *Midweek*, and writes regularly for *The Times*. She lives with her husband Paul Heiney and children Nicholas and Rose on a working farm in Suffolk.

Libby Purves

Farming

All You Need to Know

Illustrated by
George Buchanan

PUFFIN BOOKS

PUFFIN BOOKS

Published by the Penguin Group
Penguin Books Ltd, 27 Wrights Lane, London W8 5TZ, England
Penguin Books USA Inc., 375 Hudson Street, New York, New York 10014, USA
Penguin Books Australia Ltd, Ringwood, Victoria, Australia
Penguin Books Canada Ltd, 10 Alcorn Avenue, Toronto, Ontario, Canada M4V 3B2
Penguin Books (NZ) Ltd, 182–190 Wairau Road, Auckland 10, New Zealand

Penguin Books Ltd, Registered Offices: Harmondsworth, Middlesex, England

First published 1992
10 9 8 7 6 5 4 3 2 1

Printed in England by Clays Ltd, St Ives plc
Filmset in Monophoto Times

Contents

1 How Farms Began

When you go out into the country, look at the scenery. What do you see? There are trees and hedges and a pattern of fields. Some of these fields are very big; some are small. In winter they might be brown and bare, in spring and summer full of growing crops. There are animals: cows, sheep, horses. You might be lucky enough to see some of the pigs which are raised outdoors, and the strange, arched, silvery houses they live in, looking like spaceships that have just landed. There are tractors and big machines working on the fields – sometimes when a tractor is ploughing, a flock of seagulls follows it up and down the field, dive-bombing the new furrows to catch the earthworms by surprise. A network of narrow country lanes and footpaths joins all the fields and cottages and big farmhouses together.

The countryside doesn't naturally look like this. Everywhere in the world, except in the deserts, the highest mountains and deepest jungles, human beings have changed the landscape. However beautiful and natural it looks, the scenery you see has been created by people working with nature: farmers! In recent times, some farmers have interfered too much with nature, and when this happens they have to think again about the best way to do things. But the history of our landscape is the history of farming, and it is something to be proud of.

THE FIRST FARMERS

Thousands of years ago, Britain and all of northern Europe were covered in thick forest. People lived by gathering wild berries and hunting wild animals. When they ran out of food, they simply moved on. This way of life is called nomadic: there are still tribes in the world who live as nomads. In North America, the Indians lived like this until the settlers came. They followed the herds of wild

buffalo across the hundreds of miles of plain, camping in tents.

This nomadic way of life may have been happy, but it was hard. In winter, people often ran out of food. Gradually, they came to the idea that instead of going out looking for food, they could raise it themselves by growing plants near their home, and taming animals for food. This was the beginning of farming. It was the beginning of our civilization too. Once people settled down in one place and were sure of having enough food without going off hunting for it, they could begin to build villages, towns and cities. The word 'farm' means 'something set firm'. Life could become much more firm and organized once farming was invented.

For those first farmers, the two parts of the job were just the same as they are now: TILLING and GRAZING.

TILLING

This means preparing the soil so that crops can grow. To do this, they first had to cut down some trees. It is believed that the word 'field' means 'the place which has been felled' – where the trees were cut down. People did this job even before the Iron Age: they cut down trees with axes made of flint. Look at a big tree, and look at a sharp stone, and you can see what hard work that must have been.

But that wasn't all. Next time you are in a park or garden, look at the ground under the trees and imagine what you get

when you cut down trees and dig out the stumps. It isn't a useful field at all. The soil is hard, perhaps stony, and full of plants which are useless for food – weeds and brambles! Seeds can't grow when the earth is too hard and squashed down. The little roots can't take hold, and the growing shoots can't push big clods of earth out of the way. Also the weeds, which are tough, grow up so fast that they steal all the nourishment from the soil, and block out the light from the crop.

So you have to till the soil before you can plant the precious seeds you have collected. You must dig up the surface until all the weeds are uprooted, and stir up the soil so that it is crumbly and airy. Try doing this, with a nail-file or a sharp stone, and see the fresh brown earth appearing under the tired, weedy, hard surface. Early farmers had to invent tools to do this job. The most basic is a sharp stick, which men and women used as well as their hands. Then they made rakes, and later ploughs and harrows which oxen or horses could pull. Some of them learned to save themselves work by taming wild pigs and letting them rootle up the soil with their noses.

Once the soil is tilled, the seeds can be

planted and they will grow – but they need help. They need nourishment, water and sunshine. They also need protection from their enemies – weeds and thieving birds! When men and women were first learning to be farmers, they must have had one failure after another. But every disaster taught them something. For instance:

● If seeds were stolen by birds, they had to invent ways of frightening them off. The very best way was to use children, because they know how to be noisy! Up till a hundred years ago, children were often kept off school in the spring to act as bird-scarers, running up and down the fields all day, banging sticks together. These days children have to go to school (and, anyway, many of the fields are far too big). So you might hear the bang! of an automatic bird-scaring machine, or see

a scarecrow, or some ragged old plastic bags fluttering in the wind. Some farmers have a dead bird pegged out on a post to make the others think it is dangerous to come down. Sometimes you even see a kite, shaped like a hawk, flying over a field to fool the birds into thinking that a bird of prey is threatening them.

● When there was a dry spell, the young plants died from lack of moisture. So the first farmers learned how to water the fields – this is called irrigation. In a dry season, you will see sprinklers going in the fields all day. In many hot countries, nothing could grow at all without irrigation, and machines have been invented to get water to every part of the crop.

● But if it rained too hard, the ground grew soggy and young plants were washed away. So farmers learned another skill: drainage. They dug ditches for the water to run harmlessly away.

● When the weeds started to take over the crop, the lesson was about weed control. At first, they hoed out the young weeds by hand. Later, other methods were invented, including chemical weedkillers.

● But even if the farmers protected their crops, they might find after three or four seasons that the plants came up weakly and gave less food. The soil itself became less able to support life – less fertile. If you take out all the nourishment in it and don't replace it, the earth becomes exhausted. So farmers discovered one of the most important lessons of all: that they must help the soil's fertility. They found many natural things made good fertilizers as they rotted down: animal dung, bird-droppings, even seaweed. There are rocky islands in the far north of Europe where the soil is very fertile today, because thousands of years ago people carried seaweed up from the shore and spread it out on the fields to make the earth thicker and more nourishing for plants.

But tilling and growing plants is only half the farming story. The other half is:

GRAZING

When the hunters were out looking for food, sometimes they would find a young animal that had lost its mother. They would bring it home, perhaps to amuse their own children. They found out that if you look after young animals and get them used to human beings, the animals stay tame and will produce their young close by, so there is no longer any need to hunt.

Gradually the grass-eating animals were
brought home to the farm: sheep, pigs and
cattle. The farmers learned more skills:

● To stop the animals getting away, they
built fences.
● To feed the animals in winter, when
there was no grass growing, they learned
to save up some root crops and to dry
grass to make hay.
● They also learned that if you keep the
same group of animals, and go on mating
the males with the females in that one
group, generation after generation, things
will go wrong. The young ones will be
born weaker and weaker, and often with
illnesses. You have to bring in new rams,
or bulls, or boars, to improve the breed.

This is the skill of breeding, and today champion breeders, who produce the very finest young animals, can win big prizes at shows.

It took many thousands of years for people to learn all these skills – tilling, planting, fertilizing the soil, protecting crops and domesticating animals. They were inventing the art of farming. Even today we are still making new discoveries.

Until the Second World War, most farms were 'mixed' – with animals as well as crops. It was a useful system, because the animals' dung provided manure for the crops, and in the winter the cattle, sheep and pigs could be fed on food which was grown on the farm. Today, because it is easier to transport food on lorries, some farms only grow crops. They have no animals at all. These are called arable farms. Others just raise one kind of animal in large quantities. So you can get a pig farm, or a sheep farm, or a chicken farm. You can farm deer (you need very high fences to stop them jumping out!) or llamas or ostriches. There are even fish farms, raising captive salmon or trout in ponds and pens, or snail farms, growing edible snails!

2 The Arable Farming Year

Many of the farms that can be seen on a train or car journey through the countryside will be arable farms – farms with no animals. Arable farmers grow plants for food and other uses, by cultivating the soil and planting seeds. On modern arable farms, fields can sometimes be very large, and huge, complicated-looking machines work on the land. But if you look closely at the work the machines are doing, you'll find it has hardly changed for hundreds of years.

THE PLOUGH

Ploughing is usually done in the autumn. Farmers use the plough to turn the soil

17

over, so that weeds are buried and fresh soil is brought to the surface. It is in this fresh soil that the seeds are planted. The soil needs to be fresh, so that the growing crops can get the food they need from it, and it must be free of weeds, so that the young tender crops don't get robbed of food and sunlight by tough and useless plants.

A plough works by cutting a slice of earth, called a furrow, and turning it over. This is done by using a curved piece of steel, so that the soil which was at the bottom of the furrow comes to the top.

Ploughs were invented about 300 years ago, and at first oxen (strong cattle) pulled them. Later, people found that horses were cleverer and just as strong. But oxen and horses can usually cut only one furrow at a time, about twenty centimetres wide. To plough a whole field, a farmer had to drive the horses and plough up and down the field, turning furrow after furrow till it was all ploughed. To plough one acre (half a hectare) would take all day, and the farmer and horses would have to walk eleven miles (seventeen kilometres).

Look at a map, find a town seventeen kilometres from where you live and imagine walking that distance every day, guiding a heavy plough by its handles.

Later, people experimented with steam-ploughing, but steam-engines are very heavy, and before rubber was invented with which to make big wide wheels, the machines sank into the earth. With one system, there was an engine at either end of the field and wires between them, and the plough travelled along these wires!

Nowadays, tractors pull ploughs. With their big rubber tyres, they don't get bogged down easily in soft ground, and they have enormous pulling strength. Tractors have got bigger and bigger in the last fifty years, and so have the ploughs that they pull. A farmer can now plough seven or eight furrows at once, which is much faster than any horse could walk. Instead of ploughing just one acre a day, about thirty can be ploughed.

THE HARROW

Ploughing brings fresh soil to the surface, but it is not yet ready for the planting of seeds. The surface would be too lumpy – some seed would tumble between the clods of earth and be lost, and the rest would lie on top and be stolen by birds, or else rot away in the rain. Seeds like a smooth surface on which to lie, where they can snuggle between small grains of earth. So the next job the farmer has to do is to prepare what is called a seed-bed.

This is done with a harrow. A harrow is a giant rake, rather like the one gardeners

use. It has sharp fingers of iron or steel bolted on to a frame. By dragging the harrow across the ploughed field, the farmer can split all the clods into much smaller chunks of earth. If it is done for long enough, all the lumps will be broken down almost to dust. But the farmer must be careful: some seeds need a coarse seed-bed and others need a very fine one, almost like sand. Usually, the smaller the seed, the finer the seed-bed must be.

SOMETHING TO DO • SOMETHING TO DO

Look at some seeds: the kind you eat, like sunflower or pumpkin seeds, or the kind they sell for growing flowers at home. How many different sizes can you find? You could try planting the same kind in different seed-beds to see what happens – put one in fine soil, another in clods of earth, another in very stony soil. Which sprouts best?

Like ploughs, harrows are very ancient farming-tools which have changed little for centuries. But in recent years, the power-harrow has been invented. The machine is built so that the tractor can spin the harrow spikes as it goes up and down the field. It works very well, and the farmer only has to drive over the field once. If you see a tractor being driven slowly over a field with rough ground in front and smooth ground appearing behind, a power-harrow is probably being used. It looks almost as if the land is being ironed!

SEED-DRILL

Now to plant the seed, the farmer uses a seed-drill, a kind of planting-machine. Before the drill was invented, gangs of people had to march up and down fields with sticks, called dibbers. They would stab them into the ground and drop a seed into the hole they had just made. It was very slow work. Try it and see how soon you get fed up!

The seed-drill plants automatically by feeding individual seeds down tubes. At the end of the tubes are coulters (knives) which cut very thin trenches in the earth, no deeper than a centimetre. The seed drops

into this trench. There are several of these coulters side by side, and so a seed-drill can sow twenty or thirty rows at a time. It can work very quickly and huge fields can be sown in a day. The first drills were pulled by horses, but today tractors pull them. Because the seed is sown with a seed-drill, farmers hardly ever talk about sowing seed – they talk about 'drilling' it.

Once the seed is planted, the field may have to be rolled with a big roller pulled by a plough, to make sure the soil is pressed down firmly around it. Now the seed can get the moisture and food it needs to grow (provided you keep the birds off). Then the farmer can rest for a bit. But not for long.

The crop may need extra fertilizers to nourish the growing plants. The natural fertilizer is farmyard manure, or other animal and plant products, but more often chemical fertilizers are used. These will be spread with another machine, and at some point in the season a sprayer will be used too.

SPRAYS

Sprays are chemical mixtures invented to help farmers grow more crops on the same amount of land. Without help from sprays, a modern farmer might only get ten tonnes of food from a field. With the help of chemicals, thirty tonnes could be harvested from that same field. The chemicals kill weeds which threaten the crop – these are called weedkillers or herbicides. Other sprays – pesticides – poison insects which might attack the plants. Others stop diseases which growing plants can catch. Some of these chemicals are very dangerous and when farmers use them, the law says they have to wear special suits like spacesuits to protect themselves.

A spraying-machine has long arms called booms, with nozzles attached. From these nozzles a fine spray is blown on to the fields. If you are near a field which is being sprayed, you should move away or close the car window, because some sprays can make you ill. Farmers are not allowed to spray when the wind is very strong and might carry the poison far across the countryside.

HARVESTING

Once the crop has grown and ripened, it is time for the harvest to begin. Before harvesting-machinery was invented, men and women used to cut the corn by hand using a scythe, tie it into bundles and carry these back to the farmyard. To get the grains of corn out, they had to hit the stalks with a stick called a flail. Next time you are in the country and see a field of

corn, imagine how hard that job must have been, and how long it must have taken. It is called threshing, or thrashing.

Later, threshing-machines were invented and powered by steam-engines. But there were still two things to do: mowing the corn, and then threshing it. Nowadays, the two jobs are combined in a:

COMBINE HARVESTER

A 'combine' gets its name because it can do all the harvesting operations with one big machine. It cuts the crop, and then separates the useful part from the waste. If it is wheat, the farmer will want the ears of wheat to send to the miller to be made into bread. So the combine removes the ears of wheat and saves them, and drops the waste straw back on to the ground.

This straw is a problem for the modern arable farmer because there is no use for it. Remember, arable farms have no animals, so the straw can't be used to provide beds for them in the winter, or to cut up into chaff which they can eat. Some of it is baled up, but the rest must be got rid of. Farmers used to burn it – this was called stubble-burning – but that is now being discouraged. It caused some pollution, and it killed a lot of wildlife because the small animals could not get out of the way of the fire. Now farmers have to plough their straw back into the land. And with the ploughing, the arable farmer's year has started again.

3 Crops on the Farm

~FRESH GREEN ORANGES~
FROM SCOTLAND

The most important decision a farmer has to make is about which crops to grow. It depends on three things:

THE CLIMATE

This means the weather you normally get in your part of the world. It would be silly to try and grow oranges in the north of Scotland. The weather is too cold and wet and the oranges would never ripen. But in southern Spain, where oranges grow well, it would be a waste of time to try and grow cabbages or potatoes. Both these vegetables need lots of moisture, so they do best where there is a reliable rainfall.

Another good example is maize. It is

grown in much of Europe, and is a fodder crop – one that is used to feed animals. Some maize is grown for people to eat, and that is called sweetcorn. Maize only grows in fairly warm climates and so it does well in most of central Europe and in the very south of England. But as you go north, you find little maize because the weather is often too cool for the maize to ripen.

So climate is very important in choosing a crop.

THE SOIL

There are different kinds of soil. Some types of soil are very sandy. In fact, some fields in parts of Britain are almost as sandy as a seaside beach. The trouble with sandy soil is that it doesn't hold moisture very well.

Try pouring water into a bucket of sand with holes in the bottom. It soon drains away. The same thing happens when it rains on a sandy field. The moisture disappears, and it also washes away many important plant foods from the soil. That is why a lot of the sandy land in Britain used to be heathland, covered with bracken and gorse.

But sandy land – known as 'light' land –

is very good for growing carrots, because
as the growing carrot digs deeper into the
soil, it finds it easy to push through. In a
lumpy soil it gives up pushing, and that is
why you sometimes see carrots twisted into
funny shapes. So if your farm had sandy
soil, you might think of growing carrots.
Potatoes would be quite good too, if you
could provide lots of moisture by irrigating
(watering) the land. Grass will also grow
on sandy soil, but in a very hot, dry
summer the heat of the sun will dry the
grass until it dies.

Some soils are 'heavy'. They have a lot
of clay in them – sticky, lumpy stuff like
modelling clay. Clay is useful because, as

SOMETHING TO DO • SOMETHING TO DO

To test if soil is heavy, take a handful of earth
and add a little water to it, and see if you can
roll it into a sausage. Can you? And if you
press it into a ball, does it stay that shape? If it
does, you can bet you have got a soil with lots
of clay in it.

you have just discovered, it holds moisture. It doesn't drain away like it does on sandy soil. If you had a bucket of clay soil and poured water on to it, you would find the water would sit there. So for crops that need a good supply of moisture, like corn, clay soils are best. And because they hold the water, they also keep the plant foods and minerals which make them fertile.

The only trouble with clay soil is that it can get very muddy in the winter, and farmers may not be able to take heavy tractors on to their fields because they will get bogged down.

There are other types of soils, but they are all mixtures of sandy soils and clay soils. Which sort of soil a farmer has helps in the decision about which crops to grow.

THE MARKET

Whatever the farmer grows, he has to sell. He needs to get enough money to live on, after he has paid back the cost of the seed, and the fuel for the machinery, and the sprays and fertilizers.

Wheat

Wheat is probably the most important arable crop, because from wheat the miller can make flour to turn into bread. In most of the world, bread is an important food and it is often called 'the staff of life'. The farmer can choose from many different kinds of wheat. Some will produce grain

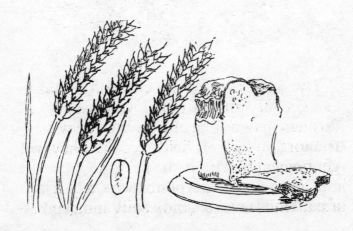

that will mill into the very finest flour –
the farmer gets paid most for these kinds.
Others will not be so good, and this wheat
will go to make animal feed. There are
also biscuit-making wheats which the
farmer will sell to the biscuit factories.

If you are visiting a farm, ask if you can
have one ear of wheat. Take it to pieces and
find the hard grain – the useful bit – and see
how much is left. There is a lot. So when the
miller has removed the most nutritious part
of the grain from the wheat, there is a lot of
waste – but this can be useful. For example,
it can be made into bran which is fed to
horses, and also a floury stuff called
middlings which is fed to pigs.

Barley

After wheat, barley is the next most
important crop. You can always tell a field
of barley because it grows with long spikes

sticking out of the top like cats' whiskers, and when it blows around in the wind, it is like watching the bristles of a brush sway from side to side.

Barley is grown in the same way as wheat: both crops can be planted in either the autumn or spring. They are harvested when ripe, and have turned from green to golden. In Britain, harvest usually happens in August.

Again, there are different kinds of barley for different jobs. The very best goes to the malting industry to make beer or whisky. Less high-quality barley is fed to animals, and fattens them up very quickly. It can also be ground into meal for pigs. We eat it too: sometimes there is barley in home-made soup (the pearl-like blobs with a black dot in the middle). This is called pearl barley and is another branch of the barley family.

Oats

Oats are not grown as widely as they used to be. But in difficult growing areas, like the north of Scotland or the Western Isles, where the summers can be wet and cold, oats always do well. That is why porridge became such an important food in Scotland, because they could always grow the oats to make it. Oats are also the very best kind of food for horses. But they have lots of other uses too: you can make cardboard and paper from the husk which is left after the milling process.

Rye

This was always thought of as a poor farmer's crop, because it would produce well even on very poor land, even if given very little attention. Two hundred years ago, vast amounts of rye were grown, but

now there is hardly any. That is because farmers have got better at growing wheat and barley, which make better bread. Try some rye bread. It is dense, heavy bread and although it is eaten in eastern Europe and Sweden, most British people don't really like it. However, there has been a fashion lately for wheat bread with a few grains of rye in it, and so more rye is being grown. If the rye is cut the old-fashioned way with a mower, instead of a combine, the stalks (rye straw) are very good for thatching houses.

Sugar-beet

When you see sugar-beet growing, it is difficult to imagine how a field of green leaves and knobbly roots could turn into white sugar – but it does! All our sugar used to come from sugar-cane, which only grows in the very hot climates of the West Indies and southern America. Now sugar-beet, grown in Britain, is the main source of our sugar.

The beet itself is the plant's root. It is the size of a football and can be quite knobbly. When it is lifted from the ground in October, the green leaves are cut off and can be fed to sheep. The beet is then taken to factories which specialize in extracting the sugar. After the sugar has been removed, a pulp is left over. This is dried, pressed into pellets and makes good animal feed. There is not much waste with sugar-beet.

Rape

If you see fields of bright yellow flowers in May, you are looking at fields of rape. Rape is grown for the oil that its seeds contain. The farmer plants the seed in the autumn and lets it grow all winter. Unfortunately, pigeons are very fond of it when there is little else for them to eat, so you might hear regular gunshots coming from farms in the winter. These shots don't actually come from guns: there is a machine which creates a controlled gas explosion every minute or so, to scare the pigeons away. It doesn't always work, because the birds get used to it!

The rape grows through the spring and forms its vivid yellow flowers in May. Then the plant goes to seed, and it is these seeds that the farmer must harvest. This is done with a combine harvester in August and the seeds, which look like tiny black ball-bearings, are sent to a factory where they are crushed. The rape-seed oil is squeezed from them and this is used to make margarine and cooking oils.

Seeds

You might wonder where all the seeds come from which farmers buy. Some farms, instead of selling their crop for food, sell it for seed. There are also scientific farms, which experiment with cross-breeding different plants to get better types that can resist disease and grow extra quickly. Then the seeds are sold to farmers.

New kinds of crops are always being developed, and new uses for them too. Scientists even say that there may be a way of making fuel for cars out of spare corn!

Market Gardening

When a farmer grows only vegetables – carrots, potatoes, cucumbers, courgettes, tomatoes, cabbages, and so on – it is

sometimes called 'market gardening'.
Market gardens are usually smaller than
farms and need more people per acre to
work on them, to keep weeds down and
pick vegetables by hand.

Fruit Farms

Especially in southern Britain, there are
farms which only grow fruit, or hops for
beer-making, or even flowers. They are
often run by very few people all year, and
temporary workers are hired for the picking
season, when there is far more work. In
the old days, families of gypsies would
travel from farm to farm in time for the
hop-picking or strawberry-picking season.

4 Animals on the Farm

A FARMING ARGUMENT

Everywhere in farming you will hear arguments about whether it is good or bad to be 'intensive'. Intensive farming is about getting results as quickly and as economically as possible, just as a factory does. An intensive farmer fattens cattle very fast, in yards or sheds, and feeds them concentrated foods instead of grass and hay. The same sort of system is often used with chickens – they call them battery hens – and with pigs. It produces a lot of food, very fast and very efficiently, so this food is cheaper in the shops. But intensive farming has its disadvantages: it isn't as pleasant for the animals, or for the people who look after them. Animals kept huddled together indoors often get diseases, and need extra medicines to keep them healthy. And the feed they eat takes energy to produce.

Some farmers are turning away from intensive systems, and working in a more traditional way. Many of them are also practising 'organic' cultivation, without chemical fertilizers and weedkillers. It seems a very good idea, but remember that food produced in this way takes more work and more time, and so costs more than intensively reared meat. As you read on about 'intensive' farming methods, decide what you think of them. From the beginning of time, farmers have had to change their environment to grow food, but how far should they go? And is it worth paying more to farmers who don't use intensive methods?

CATTLE

When you see a quiet black-and-white cow in a field, it is hard to imagine that she belongs to the same family as the bison, the wild buffalo and the yak. But even among breeds of cattle in Europe, there are great differences. There are the small,

41

JERSEY FRIESIAN

HIGHLAND

BEEF SHORTHORN

gentle Jersey cows, the black-and-white Friesians, the Highland Cattle with their long, shaggy fringes and sharp horns, the stocky Shorthorns – all members of the same family and descended from the same prehistoric cattle who lived five million years ago in Asia. They have a 'cloven hoof' – actually, it is two toes with a hoof each and a gap between them – which shows that they have even more distant relatives: the hippopotamus, the camel and the pig also have cloven hoofs.

The differences between types of cattle are due to breeding. Over the centuries, dairy farmers would choose to keep and mate the cows which produced most milk, and beef farmers would choose animals which were the right shape to produce good meat. They could also breed for other qualities: in hilly areas without much grass, you need strong, hardy cattle which can clamber over rocks and live on little food. In places where the grass grows thick and lush, you need a more placid cow which won't waste her energy on roaming around, but will calmly produce good calves and plentiful milk. And if you want to use them as oxen, to pull ploughs and carts, as they still do in some parts of Europe, you need a strong, willing animal.

Dairy Cattle
These are cows kept to give milk. Usually they are Friesian Holsteins (black and white), Ayrshires or brown Guernsey or Jersey cows. Their life is very simple. They

eat grass in summer and come into the farmyard or barn to eat hay, silage or cereals in the winter. Cows have a stomach with four compartments! This means they can eat their food, store it in a compartment called the rumen, and then bring it back to their mouth and chew it thoroughly again. This is called 'chewing the cud'. So if you see a cow chewing busily when there is no food in sight, that is what she is up to. It is a busy life too: an adult cow eats up to twenty kilograms of food a day, and must drink at least thirty litres of water. When she is giving milk, she might need more than one hundred litres!

CALVING

A female is called a heifer until her first calf is born. At around two years old, the heifer is 'served' – made pregnant for the first time. Either she mates with a bull, or she is made pregnant by 'AI' – artificial insemination – when sperm taken from a good bull is put inside her body by a specially trained operator. Artificial insemination has been a great help to breeders, because it means that a fine bull can become the father of thousands of calves, without having to travel up and down the country mating with the cows.

But some farmers still prefer the natural way.

The cow will only get pregnant if she is served at the right time, when she is 'bulling'. This only happens once every three weeks, so the farmer must keep a sharp eye out for the sign that the cow is ready. Often a bulling cow will bellow and gallop around excitedly in the field.

A little over nine months later, her calf is born. Sometimes the farmer, or the vet, has to help if the calf is going to be born in a difficult position. Straight away, the calf gets up and begins to suck its mother's milk. This first milk is very important for all young animals: it is called colostrum, and gives useful protection against illness.

MILKING

A dairy calf is usually taken away from its mother very soon, and fed from a bucket by the farmer. It has to be taught how to eat from a bucket. As the mother is not feeding her calf, it means that she can be milked. If the farmer goes on milking her twice every day, she will go on giving milk for nearly nine months after the calf is born – far longer than the calf would need to suck. Today the milking is usually done by machines. In a modern milking-parlour the cow goes into a stall where her feed is waiting, has her udder washed and then a cluster of suckers, called the milk-bag, is

fitted to the teats on her udder. The machine milks the cow in about five minutes, and the milk goes through a pipeline to a big storage tank, where it is cooled. Later a milk-tanker calls and empties the tank. In some very modern milking-parlours, the cows stand on a big rotating platform with the milkers in the middle. But the most common design is the herringbone-parlour, where all the cows on one side are milked first, and then those on the other.

Even though modern milking seems so mechanical and scientific, cows still have feelings. Nature produces the milk for a calf, not a machine, to suck and it is natural for a cow to be happy and calm when she is feeding her own calf. Her contented feeling helps the 'let-down reflex', which lets the milk flow: a nervous, unhappy cow can clench her muscles so that her milk won't flow freely. So herdsmen, who look after cows and milk them, must be calm, friendly, quiet people. In some milking-parlours they play soothing classical music to the cows – and, strangely enough, it makes the cows give more milk!

Sometimes calves do stay with their mothers, and when they do they grow faster and are stronger. This is called a suckler herd. On very small farms, it is possible for the calf to feed from its mother, and the farmer to be able to get extra milk from the cow for the family.

Milk is a valuable food, both on its own and when it has been made into cheese, butter or yoghurt. On some farms they keep their own milk instead of sending it off in a tanker, and they make their own cheeses and yoghurt and ice-cream right there on the farm.

Beef Cattle

These cows are kept to give meat. They are often of different breeds to dairy cattle, such as Beef Shorthorns, Aberdeen Angus and Herefords. The bulls are chosen for the quality of meat they produce (these days, many people prefer the meat to be very lean, with hardly any fat in it at all). The male calves born to dairy cows are also reared for meat.

The traditional way to bring up beef calves is to let them graze in the open fields for two years or a little longer before slaughter. Today, however, many farmers prefer an intensive system in which they feed the animals indoors, or in yards, on special concentrated foods. With this system, the animals might be ready for the

butcher in just one year, producing a large
quantity of lean meat. Veal calves are fed
on a special diet, and are killed at three
months old.

However, many people are beginning to
think that the old-fashioned style of beef,
from grass-fed cattle which have lived two
years in the open, actually tastes better.
Since it also gives the animals a longer,
pleasanter life and means that the
countryside is kept full of beautiful grazing

meadows and marshes instead of big ugly sheds, this system is becoming more popular again.

SHEEP

Some people say that all our great cities have been built on the back of a sheep! In a way, it is quite true. Sheep were one of the first animals used by people, and you will find traces of them for thousands of years back, on land stretching from the far northernmost islands of Europe right down into Asia. Their wool has clothed us and made us blankets, their meat has fed us and (almost as important, in some places) their grazing and their droppings have helped to fertilize land for growing crops. Another farmers' name for sheep is 'the

golden hoof'. Not only do sheep fertilize the land, but the way their small light hoofs tread it down is actually good for preparing the soil for crops. Cows and horses churn up the earth with their hoofs, while sheep pat it neatly down. Bigger animals often spoil a grass field in wet weather, but sheep hardly ever do.

How many different kinds of sheep have you seen? There are twenty to thirty kinds in Britain alone – from the dark, goaty-looking Soay sheep in northern Scotland to the fat, black-faced Suffolks. And, of course, shepherds often 'cross-breed' them, putting a male (the ram) of one breed with a different flock of female sheep (ewes).

But you can usually tell whether you are looking at an upland sheep, which lives in harsh, hilly climates in the north, or a lowland sheep. The upland sheep have extra-thick wool, and have to be very nimble and good at climbing, and very hardy. Often they are trapped in snowdrifts for days, and they have to put up with biting cold and gales as well as rain. Upland sheep run very fast – shepherds and their dogs find them a great challenge to control!

A lowland sheep is usually fatter and slower. It has plenty of good grass to eat, and doesn't have to wander far and wide like a mountain sheep, or eat coarse food like heather and tough grasses. Lowland sheep often have twin lambs, or even triplets, because they can easily make enough milk to feed them. Upland sheep normally have just one lamb.

Mating

Sheep know, in their bodies, what time of year it is. Most breeds will only mate in the short days of autumn and winter. This is nature's way of trying to make sure that the lambs arrive in the spring, when there is plenty of food and warmth. But farmers know that if they can get lambs born early – even in the depths of winter – those lambs will be old enough for market earlier in the year, and so will fetch more money. On the other hand, if ewes are feeding their

lambs in the winter when there is no fresh grass, they will have to be given a lot of expensive fodder. So the farmer must decide how early to put the ram in with the ewes, depending on when the lambs are to be born. It takes a sheep 147 days from mating to giving birth. Work out when you'd have to put the ram in, if you wanted lambs born in March!

It is useful for the shepherd to know when the ram has mated with each ewe. So the ram wears a harness, with a crayon fixed to the chest – and when he mates with a ewe, the ewe gets a scribble of colour on her back. If the shepherd changes the crayon every week, it can be worked out just how recently a ewe was mated, and so which week her lamb will be born.

Lambing

Sheep can live out of doors all year long so long as somebody takes them hay or concentrated feed-blocks in the winter when the grass stops growing. But ewes which are going to have their lambs in the cold weather are usually brought indoors, or into a sheltered farmyard, during the worst of the weather. This also means that the pastures have a chance to recover.

When the lambs are due, the shepherd keeps a close watch. Often the ewe manages to give birth by herself. The front hoofs of the lamb come out first, then the head, then the rest – rather like a little diver. But if the lamb is the wrong way round, or has its legs bent back inside the ewe, the shepherd has to put his hand very gently into the birth passage and help it to turn the right way. When there are twin lambs they quite often get tangled up together, and a very skilled hand is needed from the shepherd. But it is a great moment for the ewe and the shepherd when the lamb flops out, quite safe, and stands on its long legs to reach up and suck its mother's milk. The ewe sniffs and licks and nuzzles often at her lamb in the first few hours, and defends it if another sheep, or a person, tries to interfere.

Occasionally, especially if she is in a crowded pen with a lot of other ewes, a mother gets confused and rejects her own lamb by butting it away. Or sometimes there is an orphan lamb to be fed, and a ewe whose own lamb has died, and the shepherd wants to put them together. If the ewe won't let the lamb feed, she may have her head put gently in a fixed frame, called an 'adopter', so that she stands still

while the lamb feeds. She can still feed and lie down, but she can't butt the lamb. After two or three days, she gets so used to the lamb she accepts it as her own.

If there is no ewe to feed a lamb, or if it is very sickly, the shepherd or one of the family will have to bottle-feed it. Since young lambs have to be fed every three or four hours at least, day and night, it is hard work. Bottle-fed lambs are very tame, and follow people around. When they become full-grown sheep, this can be a nuisance: often a hand-reared lamb which has been put back in the flock will be the one which teaches all the rest to escape through the hedge, and will come back to the farmhouse for an unexpected visit!

Growing Up

Young lambs usually have their tails cut short ('docked') by having a tight rubber ring fitted so that the end loses its blood supply and falls off. There is a good reason: otherwise their back-end gets very dirty with their dung, and flies lay their eggs there. When the maggots come out of the eggs, they start to eat the lamb's flesh. The rubber ring does not seem to bother the lamb at all, so while it may look uncomfortable, it is probably the kindest thing to do.

Out in the field with their mothers, the young lambs frisk and play and learn to eat the fresh grass. Like cows, they have an extra stomach, the rumen, and eating grass helps this to develop healthily. The

shepherd doesn't have to feed them now, but must still be wary: foxes love to carry off young lambs at night, and magpies may attack them and peck their eyes.

Shearing
When the days grow hotter, the sheep feel very uncomfortable in their long fleeces. The time has come to shear them, and the wool is a useful crop in itself. Most shepherds now use electric shears, but it is

still a very skilled job to get the fleece off in one piece, tidy and clean. With very big flocks, like those in Australia, shearing gangs are used. These rove around the country doing nothing but shear sheep. Small flocks might be done just by the farmer. Shearing is also a good time to check the animals' feet: if you don't clip

sheeps' hoofs regularly, they get a disease
called foot-rot. Later in the year, all sheep
must be 'dipped', by law. They are driven
through a chemical bath to kill off any
parasites, insects and skin diseases they
might have.

Sheepdogs

Although sheep cause quite a lot of work,
people grow very fond of their flocks.
Shepherds have to understand how a
sheep's mind works in order to manage
them. Sheep often try to escape and
wander around where they shouldn't be.
So the shepherd's very best friend is the
sheepdog.

There are many different machines on a farm, but nobody has ever produced a machine which can do what a sheepdog does. Without these working dogs, there would be no sheep-keeping – especially in the hilly areas. It would take a dozen champion athletes to round up a flock which a dog could control quickly and without fuss. Most of our sheepdogs are Border collies as they are quick and intelligent.

Watch how sheepdogs work, in real life or on television. They have to obey orders or whistles meaning 'Go left – go right – stop – lie down – move forward – look back'. 'Look back' is necessary because the dog may not have noticed that it has left one or two sheep behind.

Sheep have a natural fear, inherited from their ancestors, of being hunted by wolves. This means they will always bunch together and turn away from a moving dog. The faster the dog goes, the faster they will move. If the dog lies down, they will stand still and face it, waiting to see what it will do. If it runs to one side of the flock, they will move away in the other direction. They are not terrified of the dog – if they were, they would panic and run for miles, which would be of no help to the shepherd. They are just nervous enough to obey. Occasionally one sheep gets cheeky and tries to defy the dog: a good dog will run up to it and threaten to nip its nose.

Imagine the chaos if the dog didn't obey the shepherd, or the sheep didn't obey the dog! Yet most of the time, one person and one dog can easily control a hundred sheep, herding them neatly from field to field, or through a narrow gate into the farmyard. The dogs love the work. One famous sheepdog lost her leg in an accident, but still manages to herd sheep by running on three legs!

Shepherds down the centuries have made up some wonderful names for types of sheep: a ram is a tup, a ram lamb is a hogg, a male lamb that has been castrated (so it can't mate) is a wether. Ewe lambs grow up to be hoggs, gimmers, or chilvers; ewes a year old are theaves, or shearlings.

SOMETHING TO DO • SOMETHING TO DO

Try to design a machine that would herd sheep as neatly and quickly as a dog does. Even if it was fast enough, how could you be sure the sheep would be just nervous enough to move away from it, but not so nervous that they panicked?

PIGS

Pigs are the most intelligent of farm animals. Their ancestors lived wild in the woodlands, and rootled around with their snouts for acorns and bulbs. Men hunted them for food. Even when pigs were first brought in to be bred on farms, they were often turned

out on to waste ground to find their own food for part of the year. They were also used as cultivators: their natural way of digging for food made them act as ploughs – even better, because at the same time they gobbled up the weeds and fertilized the land with their dung! Iron Age farmers may have used pigs as much as ploughs and hoes – the old word for a field ploughed by pigs is a 'pannage'.

Today, pigs still love to live outdoors, on ground where they can dig up grubs and plants as well as eating the food the farmer brings them. They must have a house to keep them warm in winter, though, and they organize their own housekeeping very busily. Pigs like a tidy life: if you give them plenty of straw, they make themselves comfortable beds, and each morning will throw out the straw they think is not clean enough. They never drop their dung near their bed, or their feeding-place, and in the summer they love to be kept clean with a hosepipe. Even their habit of covering themselves with mud is a sensible one: they have very delicate skins, and rolling in mud helps to protect them from sunburn.

Pigs grow fast, eat a wide range of foods and produce excellent meat which can be treated in many ways – as pork joints, sausages, spare ribs, chops, bacon and ham. In the old days, poor country people would buy a piglet, fatten it up on household scraps and live all winter off the pickled or salted meat. In many countries there are still plenty of family pigs: in China there is a saying that a family is rich if it has both a pig and a bicycle!

Today pigs have become very important animals to the farmer, and often whole farms are devoted to rearing them. Unlike sheep or cattle, they can produce huge families all year round. A young female pig – called a gilt – can be ready for

breeding at only six months old, and a
sow might have three litters a year, each
of them of ten or twelve piglets.

SOMETHING TO DO • SOMETHING TO DO

Work out how many babies a sow might have
in three years of life.

Because of all these facts, some farmers
have tried to treat pigs as machines for
producing more and more meat, as fast as
possible. Pigs have been bred to produce
larger litters, and in special body-shapes to
give good lean bacon. Most pigs in Britain
spend their whole lives indoors in big
barns. When the sows are pregnant or
feeding their piglets they are often tethered
to the floor and confined in narrow frames
which prevent them moving freely, but
which ensure that the piglets can reach the
teats whenever they like. Keeping pigs
indoors means that they use up all their
energy on growing bigger and fatter as fast
as possible, instead of wasting that energy

moving around and rootling in the ground.

This 'intensive' method has its disadvantages. The crates and tethers for sows are cruel: in Britain the government has agreed that they are, and will ban them in the future. Pigs kept close together are likely to get diseases, so they have to be fed on medicines even before they are ill. Some people believe the medicines make the meat taste worse, and even that they might be bad for humans.

There is another way to keep pigs. They can be given more space in the barns, and even toys to play with like big footballs, while still keeping them indoors. Pregnant sows must always be kept separate, though, or else they fight, so you need a lot of space. Or else you can keep pigs outdoors. More and more often pig arcs like this can

be seen in the countryside. At first the field looks like a camp of silvery huts, like the army use. But it is for an army of outdoor pigs. They roam around freely inside an electric fence, have their litters of piglets and raise them outdoors. It is not always easy for the farmer, because when it rains the field becomes a boggy mess. Also pigs can't be herded together like sheep, so each pig runs off in whatever direction it likes. But the pigs are happier and some people think the meat tastes better too.

Farrowing

When a sow is ready to give birth (three months and three weeks after she mates with the boar), she drags some straw together to make a comfortable bed, lies down, grunts a few times and out come the piglets one by one. Healthy sows hardly ever need any help with their farrowing. Each piglet gets up and finds its way round to the teats for a drink of milk: soon there are nine, ten, eleven or even twelve small piglets nuzzled up to the sow, feeding happily. At first they just rush for any teat, but after two days each piglet has its own teat and goes to the same one

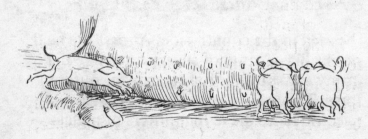

every time, just as children go to their own coat-peg in school. The strongest piglets get the best teats, nearest the sow's head – the little ones, or 'runts', have to make do with the teats lower down the body, where there is slightly less milk.

Butchering

Pigs are sensitive animals, so they should be treated with extra consideration at the end of their lives. It is important for all farm animals that they are not frightened or hurt when the time comes to go to the butcher. There are places called 'abattoirs' where the animals are killed, and good farmers make sure that the journey there is short, that the animals don't go hungry or thirsty on the way, that they aren't kept long in unfamiliar surroundings, and that they never feel any pain. At the abattoir, the animal is stunned – made completely unconscious – before it is actually killed. Then very quickly the carcass is cleaned out and hung up, ready to be cut into joints of meat.

Some people worry about killing animals for meat at all, and it is quite possible to live without meat. But if farm animals weren't bred by farmers for meat, there would hardly be any. There are no wild pigs or wild sheep

and cattle left in most of Europe. If nobody
ate meat, we would not see any lambs in the
fields, no meadows, no wide grazing-marshes
beside rivers: the countryside would change
entirely. So good farmers try to make sure
that their animals have happy lives and
calm, painless deaths. And good shoppers
keep a look-out for meat which comes from
animals raised kindly and naturally!

POULTRY

Chickens, ducks, geese and turkeys are all
poultry and are useful for eggs as well as
meat. Sometimes they are raised on special
farms which do nothing else, but they are
also part of the traditional mixed
farmyard.

Chickens

There are many breeds of chicken – in fact,
they come in almost every colour,
including green and blue! But they are all
descended from the jungle fowl, which
lived in the tropical forests of Asia many
thousands of years ago. The Chinese were
the first people to keep chickens at home,
then the habit reached the Mediterranean
countries, and it was probably 2,000
years ago that hens came to Britain.

Hens are very useful creatures. They eat scraps of almost anything, including most weeds and insects which might damage crops, and their droppings are a good fertilizer. A few farmers still use the old-fashioned system of putting hens to work as cleaners. They let a big flock live on a field for a few weeks to clean up all the weed seeds and insects before the new crop is sown.

But most chickens in our shops are raised very intensively. You might see a chicken farm which looks more like a factory, with long sheds and no green areas at all. In 'battery' houses, hens are kept in rows of wire cages, with hardly room to turn round. Their feed is delivered in measured portions down one tube, and their eggs roll away down another to be processed. Chickens raised for meat are also kept crowded together on the floor of a big building, often in half-darkness to prevent them pecking one another. At first the chicks are kept in one corner to prevent them running around and wasting their energy. Then gradually the space is widened so that at any one time they just have room to stand and crouch down, but not enough to run.

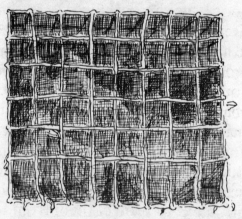

These intensive systems are very efficient. People have bred hens which can live in battery cages and lay almost 300 eggs a year. Out in a farmyard you would be lucky to get 150. The meat chickens, 'broilers', can grow big enough to be eaten after only six weeks. It is a dreary life they lead, but at least it is a short one. It means that chicken meat, and eggs, are cheap and plentiful.

But many people are unhappy about this way of raising chickens. The hens are kept healthy in their bodies, but show signs of restlessness and unhappiness. They are a long way from their natural behaviour, which is to wander around, looking for food and pecking it up busily, and to take dustbaths, flapping their wings in the dust to chase out itchy insects.

Indoor hens can develop diseases and parasites, some of which (like salmonella) can be harmful to humans. The law now insists on very careful health checks for all hens, but some farmers believe it is better to go back to the old-fashioned system, producing less food in a more natural way.

Outdoor chickens are given a run to wander about in, but are shut into a hen-house at night to protect them from foxes and stoats and other predators. They may be kept quite crowded, and are fed on special pellets made in a factory which have all the nourishment they need. Or, with a small flock, the farmer may give them more room to run around and feed them partly on scraps and the leavings of corn from the bigger animals' feed.

Chickens have a special bag in their stomach, called the gizzard, which has very strong muscles. This is where they grind up hard food, like grains of corn, but to do it they need grit. So unless they are pecking in earth, they have to be fed grit specially to do this! They also need calcium, to build strong eggshells. Sometimes they eat the old eggshells, and sometimes they are fed the ground-up shells of oysters.

There are nest-boxes where they can lay their eggs, but one disadvantage of the free-range system for the farmer is that some hens prefer to hide their eggs away in different places!

When you want hens to breed, instead of just laying eggs for the table, they must run with a male, the cockerel, for a time. Then the eggs they lay will be fertile, which means the eggs can develop into a baby chick (most eggs we eat are infertile – there is no chick embryo inside them).

SOMETHING TO DO • SOMETHING TO DO

Look at an egg. Ask an adult to break it open. What you see is the white, or albumen, and the bright yellow yolk. These will nourish the growing chick in a fertilized egg.

When she has laid her eggs, the hen goes broody. She will sit on her eggs for most of the day and night, only leaving them so that she can eat and drink. Sometimes hens go broody even if they haven't been with a cockerel, and their eggs have no chicks inside. So sometimes the farmer uses the hen's broodiness by putting her on another clutch of eggs – perhaps those of a duck which has left them (ducks are rather forgetful mothers). The hen may be surprised when ducklings hatch instead of chicks, but she still tries to look after them.

Normally, though, the hen sits on her own eggs. After three weeks the chicks begin to peck the inside of the shell, and

Last one out's chicken!

finally break out. The mother hen is very fussy and protective and leads her babies proudly around the run, teaching them to scratch and peck for food.

Turkeys
Wild turkeys first came from North America. Explorers brought them to Europe over 400 years ago. There are many different breeds, coloured bronze,

BROAD-BREASTED BRONZE

NORFOLK BLACK

BELTSVILLE WHITE.

black and white. Like chickens, they are mostly produced in big factory farms, although free-range turkeys can live very successfully and – many people think – taste better too.

Ducks and Geese

These poultry are not factory farmed. Ducks eat insects, slugs, waterfleas and grass, and also the same sort of factory-made pellets as chickens. Geese are mainly grazing birds, using up grass on verges or awkwardly shaped patches where bigger animals could not graze easily. Ducks must have a pond or ditch to swim in; geese can manage without.

Geese are excellent watchdogs, because they don't like strangers and make a very loud cackling noise if they are disturbed. They also attack sometimes. If you are on a farm visit, don't tease the geese!

5 Grass and Fields

People in towns often think that grass just grows – sometimes too fast in summer, when they keep having to mow the lawn! But grass is one of the biggest crops in the world: nearly a quarter of the world's land surface is covered in it, and is used for grazing animals. Some of it, on the hills, is entirely natural. But a great deal of grassland is cultivated, as carefully as any other crop.

Look closely at any patch of grass: you will see that not every blade is the same. When the grass is flowering, see how many different species of plants you can find in one square metre. You will be surprised. Grass is a complicated crop, and managing grassland is a science in itself. Some people spend all their lives studying it.

PERMANENT PASTURE

This is land which is always under grass. Usually what grows there is rye-grass, together with some clover and other plants in the same family. Farmers can buy special grass mixtures to suit their own soil.

TEMPORARY GRASSLAND

This is land which is sometimes used for other crops, but which is having a rest for a year or two, with grass and grazing animals, to help bring back its fertility.

Farmers have to be very careful about their grassland. If it gets too soggy, or there

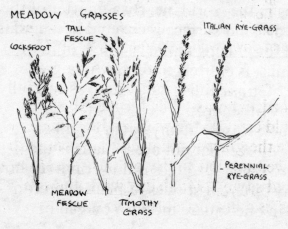

MEADOW GRASSES

TALL FESCUE

COCKSFOOT

ITALIAN RYE-GRASS

MEADOW FESCUE

TIMOTHY GRASS

PERENNIAL RYE-GRASS

is too much acid in the soil, the wrong kinds of grass will grow fastest. If heavy animals like cows and horses are put out on it in very wet weather, they will trample it so badly that the grass can't grow. If the same animals live on it year after year, the land might become infested with worms from their dung. This could get back into the animals' system.

Different animals graze differently. Cows like long grass which they wrap around their tongues and pull up; sheep have neat little teeth which crop the grass very tidily. Horses will take a dislike to certain tussocks of grass and eat all round them until the field looks untidy.

SOMETHING TO DO • SOMETHING TO DO

Look closely at a field with animals in. See the ways in which the different types of animals graze. Look at the mess cows and horses make with their hoofs and how neatly the sheep press the land down without damaging it.

HAY

This is dried grass. The farmer 'shuts up' the field early in the year, and in June, before the grass has flowered, it's cut with a mower and left to dry on the ground. The old saying 'Make hay while the sun shines' is still true: nothing is more depressing for a farmer than cutting the hay and then getting it rained on day after day. The faster it dries, the more nourishment will stay in it for the animals in winter-time.

When it is dry, it is made into bales – often big round ones which you can see in the fields in summer. Old-fashioned farmers still cart it loosely back to the farmyard and make a haystack, which is

then covered with tarpaulins. Modern farmers store it in a Dutch barn, which is a building with open sides so that the air can get through.

SILAGE

This is pickled grass (or sometimes maize or other green crops), which is used for feeding farm animals. Making silage is a

chemical process using the natural
substances in the grass. The grass is
pressed hard to get all the air out.
Sometimes this is done in a special tower,
a tall airtight cylinder of steel or concrete.
Silage is usually bright brown and has a
strong smell, but the animals like it!

FENCES

One more thing you might notice on
grassland is the way farmers enclose it, to
stop animals from straying. In areas where
there is a lot of natural rock, you will find

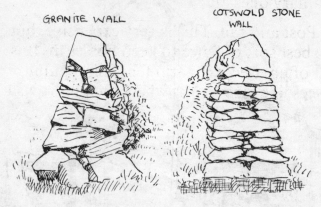

DRYSTONE WALLS

GRANITE WALL

COTSWOLD STONE WALL

stone walls: in Derbyshire and Yorkshire there are beautiful 'drystone' walls. They look as if they are just thrown together, but building them is really an art.

> **SOMETHING TO DO • SOMETHING TO DO**
> Try to build a miniature drystone wall that is strong and stable, out of pebbles. It isn't easy!

Another kind of boundary is the hedge. Hedges look natural, but they have all been planted and looked after by skilled workers. Hedge-laying is another art: the branches are bent so that they grow together and make a barrier that even the most determined sheep can't break through.

If a farmer has a fence, it could be an

ordinary one, or it could be electric. The ordinary ones are:

● Post and rail. This is very expensive, but the best sort of fence to keep horses in. It is not often used as a farm fence, except in places like farm parks where the public visit.

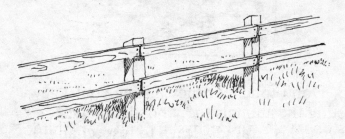

● Post and wire. This is a bit cheaper, and if it is well made it lasts for years. But if the wire breaks, animals get tangled up in it. Often one strand is made of barbed wire. This stops the animals from leaning on it or scratching themselves when they're itchy. A cow scratching herself can knock down a fence in no time.

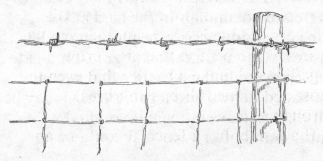

● Electric fences should always have a sign on them like this:

Don't touch, or they'll sting you! They sting the animals too, and all animals – even pigs – rapidly learn to respect an electric fence and stay where they're meant to be. Some electric fences look like tape, some look like orange string, others like ordinary post-and-wire fencing. Stop and think for a moment before you touch any fence. On footpaths there will usually be a stile you can safely climb over, or a gate to open. If you open a gate, though, **DON'T FORGET TO SHUT IT!** Even if there are no animals in the field at the time, the farmer could be planning to let some in through a different gate. Or a gate left open could bang in the wind and get damaged. If you find a gate open, it may be all right to leave it open; if you find it shut, shut it after you.

6 Farmers and the Weather

A farmer's favourite programme on the
television is the weather forecast. It
matters much more to a farmer than to
people with indoor jobs. If the ground is
wet with too much rain, the farmer won't
be able to work it because the tractors will
sink in. If it is too hard and dry, it can't
be worked either.

In the spring, a vegetable farmer
(sometimes called a market-gardener)
wants to make sure the last frost is gone
before planting some seeds which might
shoot up and be killed by the cold; a
livestock farmer is wondering whether to
put the cows out on the fields yet, because
if there is going to be a lot of rain, their

hoofs will churn up the ground and stop the fresh grass growing. He (or she, because there are plenty of women running farms) has to decide whether to risk it: he wants to put the cows out as early as possible, because it costs much more to feed them in the yard or the barn.

In summer, he needs sun to help dry the hay. In autumn, he is worried that the rain will flatten his wheat. In the winter, the farmer needs warning of snow and ice, because they make it hard to feed animals out on the fields, and can stop the milk-tanker getting through to take away his day's milk. He is always having to decide which of the many jobs to do first. So never distract a farmer who is watching the weather forecast!

7 The Changing Farm

Until forty or fifty years ago, all farms were mixed: they raised animals as well as crops, using the animals' dung as fertilizer, and fattening sheep, pigs and chickens on parts of the crop which would otherwise be wasted. A farmer was proud of being able to feed all the animals without buying in fodder from outside, and of having corn or vegetables to sell as well.

Farms were also smaller than they are today – fifty years ago a farm of one hundred acres was considered big. And because they had animals, and used horses instead of machines, they employed more people.

Today there are huge farms – two thousand acres or more – which do nothing but grow cereals, and only need three or four workers because they use big, fast machines. Often old trees and hedges have been taken out to make enormous fields for the machines to work in. Sometimes one field can be a hundred acres – the size of a whole mixed farm a century ago. All this has been made possible by the invention of machines, artificial fertilizers and other chemicals. It means that there is plenty of food, and that it is cheap for people to buy. It also means that fewer people are needed to work on the land, and their jobs are much easier. In the old days, a ploughman had to walk miles behind his horses; today his children or grandchildren can sit in a tractor cab in the warm, listening to the radio. But, as those first farmers found out

in the Iron Age, there is a price to pay for everything. It is true that the old-fashioned way of farming produced less food for every acre, and that the lives of farmworkers were tough. Sometimes bad weather, or a plague of insects or a disease, meant that a farmer's whole crop was ruined or all the animals killed. Many small farmers lost all their money and had to give up. They were not easy days.

But, on the other hand, modern farming has its problems too. Intensive systems are unnatural for animals, and can produce diseases. Putting a great deal of artificial fertilizer down to grow more and more crops can actually exhaust the land by taking away all its nourishing minerals, so that you need more and more fertilizer on the crops to make them grow.

Pulling out hedges and creating big fields can create a worse problem of soil erosion, when the top layer of the soil is washed away in winter and blown away in summer. Farm machinery uses up a lot of fuel, and so do the factories which make chemicals and animal feeds. And the very big machines which now work the land are so heavy that they squash down the soil, and then more machines – using more fuel! – have to be used to stir it up again and make it light enough for shoots to force their way up. It wouldn't be practical for everyone to go back to farming with horses, but if you get a chance, look at a field which horses have ploughed, and crumble up the earth in your hands. It feels different to tractor-ploughed earth.

LOOKING FOR A BALANCE

Farmers are always looking for a balance between natural ways and artificial ones. Sometimes they realize they have thrown out the old ways too fast because they were so excited by new machines and chemicals and quick ways of rearing animals.

ORGANIC FARMING

More and more farmers are going 'organic' – like the Prince of Wales at his own farm at Highgrove! Organic farmers don't use modern weedkillers and pesticides, but only natural fertilizers like manure or seaweed.

They won't raise animals intensively, or allow them to be fed on unnatural diets. There was a time when some factory hens were being fed on pellets which included old chicken-droppings and dead hens; and cows were fed on ground-up and processed bodies of dead sheep. This has now been stopped by law. Organic farmers would never have done it anyway.

Organic farmers need to work very hard, and be very careful, to make it work – but many of them have proved that it can succeed.

Other farmers, without turning organic, have cut down on the chemicals they use, raise all their animals outdoors, and don't pull out hedges or fill in ponds for the sake of the wildlife. A few of them have started to experiment with allowing carthorses back on to the farm, to do small jobs like carting feed out to sheep in winter.

FARMERS AND GOVERNMENTS

All these decisions which farmers have to make are not just important for them. They matter to everyone. What farmers do affects what food we eat, how good it is for us, what it tastes like, our wildlife, and how the countryside looks.

But remember something else: farmers in any country are affected by the rest of the world. If another country with a better climate, or which pays its workers less money, starts to sell your country cheaper food, then farmers at home will suffer. They will find that the price they can get for their crops goes down so much that they can't earn a living. They might have to give up farming, or switch their whole farm to a different crop. If cheap lamb was coming in, they would give up keeping sheep; if it was cheap corn, give up corn, and so on. Switching around like that might be bad for the countryside where they live, and it might be dangerous too. Suppose the foreign countries suddenly had bad weather and couldn't send us any food? There might be shortages.

So governments make farming rules. They have rules to prevent disease spreading: for instance, you have to have a special licence every time you move a pig from place to place. They have rules about the most healthy way to treat milk, and meat. And they also use government money – the money adults pay as taxes – to give farmers subsidies.

A subsidy is money paid to a farmer for raising certain kinds of crops or animals. If a government (or a club of governments, like the European Community) wants to encourage sheep-keeping, then what do they do? They pay sheepfarmers a few pounds for every ewe they own, even before it is sold. If the price of corn is low because the world has grown too much of it, the government can keep the corn-farmers going by giving them extra money for every tonne they sell cheap. When farmers live in beautiful places which are important for wildlife, governments sometimes pay them extra money not to plough up pretty riverbanks, or drain marshes. This means that the farmer can afford to do without the money he would have earned by spoiling that bit of landscape. Often, he is glad of that, because he didn't want to spoil it anyway, but couldn't keep his family unless he did.

It is very complicated for governments
to make sure that they are being fair and
encouraging the most sensible, kind,
healthy and responsible sorts of farming.
Everyone wants farming to be good for
people, wildlife and the countryside. But
farmers and politicians and ordinary
people who pay taxes are always arguing
about how to do this. Listen to the news
or read the newspapers – nearly every day
there is a farming argument.

SOMETHING TO DO • SOMETHING TO DO

If you were Prime Minister, what rules would
you like to make for farmers?

If you were a farmer, what help would you
want from the government?

It is sometimes useful to write to
Members of Parliament or Ministers of
Agriculture to point out what you think
about farming, and tell them which kinds
you think they should encourage. And
when voters elect a new government, the
most sensible ones take a good look at
how the different politicians plan to look
after farming and the countryside. Just as
sensible shoppers sometimes stop and think
where the food in their trolley is coming
from, how it has been raised, and whether

they are pleased or sorry to be supporting it.

All of us are connected with farming, just as we were back in the Iron Age, when the first farmers scratched up the earth with sharp sticks to grow food for their families. The better we understand farming, the better it will get.

Index